D0049019

Dear Parents:

Congratulations! Your child is taking the first steps on an exciting journey. The destination? Independent reading!

STEP INTO READING® will help your child get there. The program offers five steps to reading success. Each step includes fun stories and colorful art or photographs. In addition to original fiction and books with favorite characters, there are Step into Reading Non-Fiction Readers, Phonics Readers and Boxed Sets, Sticker Readers, and Comic Readers—a complete literacy program with something to interest every child.

Learning to Read, Step by Step!

Ready to Read   Preschool–Kindergarten
• big type and easy words • rhyme and rhythm • picture clues
For children who know the alphabet and are eager to begin reading.

Reading with Help   Preschool–Grade 1
• basic vocabulary • short sentences • simple stories
For children who recognize familiar words and sound out new words with help.

Reading on Your Own   Grades 1–3
• engaging characters • easy-to-follow plots • popular topics
For children who are ready to read on their own.

Reading Paragraphs   Grades 2–3
• challenging vocabulary • short paragraphs • exciting stories
For newly independent readers who read simple sentences with confidence.

Ready for Chapters   Grades 2–4
• chapters • longer paragraphs • full-color art
For children who want to take the plunge into chapter books but still like colorful pictures.

STEP INTO READING® is designed to give every child a successful reading experience. The grade levels are only guides; children will progress through the steps at their own speed, developing confidence in their reading.

Remember, a lifetime love of reading starts with a single step!

Visit us on the Web!
StepIntoReading.com
randomhousekids.com

Educators and librarians, for a variety of teaching tools, visit us at
RHTeachersLibrarians.com

ISBN 978-1-101-93680-1 (trade) — ISBN 978-1-101-93681-8 (lib. bdg.)

Printed in the United States of America

10 9 8 7 6 5 4

BUBBLE TROUBLE!

by Mary Tillworth
illustrated by Kevin Kobasic

Random House 🏠 New York

Vroom!

Blaze and his friends race through the mud.

They jump.

They splash.

Mud flies everywhere!

Time to clean up
at the Truck Wash!
Gabby tells Crusher
to press the soap button.

Crusher presses
the soap button
again and again.
Bubble trouble!

Boom!

The Truck Wash

breaks.

Blaze must find

the missing parts.

Blaze speeds
into action!
He chases
the spin brush.

Blaze throws

his tow hook.

Blaze catches
the spin brush!
He tosses it
onto his truck bed.

The bubble blasters
leave a trail
of bubbles.
Blaze follows the trail!

Blaze slips
on the soapy bubbles.
He crashes!

Blaze turns himself
into a bumper car.
Now he does not crash.
He bounces off things!

Blaze grabs
the bubble blasters
and puts them
in his truck.

Blaze and his friends
find the water sprayers
on top of a
tall building.

Crusher tries
to reach the sprayers.
Oh, no!
Crusher hits the wall!

AJ raises the ramp
for Darington and Starla.
They each grab a sprayer!

Blaze jumps
the highest.
He grabs
the third sprayer!

Blaze takes the spin brush,
bubble blasters,
and water sprayers
to Gabby.

Gabby fixes
the Truck Wash!
One by one,
the trucks drive through.

Blaze and his friends
are clean and happy.
No more bubble trouble!